Zac's Mighty Wheels and the Case of the Missing Grannies

Zac's Mighty Wheels and the Case of the Missing Grannies

By Andrea Kurth
and Braden Kurth

Illustrated by Justin Rose

Greenhouse Press

Library of Congress Number: 2022913692

Printed in the United States of America

First printing December 2022

Paperback ISBN: 978-1-7369403-4-1
Hardcover ISB: 978-1-7369403-3-4
eBook ISBN: 978-1-7369403-5-8

Kurth Books

Edited by Nadara "Nay" Merrill
www.thatgrammargal.com
and Sarah Wynne
www.littlebirdediting.co.uk
Designed by Justin Rose
www.justinrose.net

www.kurthbooks.com

For my brother Bobby, whose inspiration led me to become a special education teacher and now an author.
AK

For my wife and kids, whom I love more than anything in this world. Thank you for inspiring me to be the best artist, husband, and dad I can be.
JR

Contents

Chapter 1

Cookies

What can I do to get Mom to unground me from my Mighty Wheels?
Zac wondered as he stared up at the ceiling. She had freaked out after he flew into a flock of birds and got a bit scraped up, and now his glorious Mighty Wheels lay in the corner of his mom's room.

I can handle some pecking marks. What's the big deal? Zac thought.

Zac's wheelchair was not an ordinary wheelchair. This past

summer, he'd discovered a wishing well in the woods that transformed his wheelchair. Not only could he bounce, travel at lightning speed, and use a robo-arm that could reach as high as the tallest tree, he could also fly. His rocket boosters could blast him up as high as a plane, while his wings glided him around any object in the way. What most kids dream about, he could now do. They started calling the wheelchair Mighty Wheels, and it stuck. After defeating a giant, Zac felt like the most powerful kid in the world. His friends thought that was a stretch.

Ding dong!

Zac wheeled himself out in his old wheelchair and went to answer the door. The old chair was so slow, he felt like he was crawling. When he finally reached the front door, he flung it open. "Grandma!"

"Where is your new wheelchair?" Zac's grandma asked, giving him a tight squeeze.

"Mom thinks it's too dangerous," he replied. His grandma rolled her eyes, and they giggled as she hung up her coat.

"What do you want to do today?" his grandma asked.

"Let's make butter tarts!" Zac exclaimed.

"It's not Christmas! Butter tarts are special for Christmas, just like *my* Grandpa always made when I was young. How about chocolate chip cookies instead?" his grandma asked.

"Sounds good, as long as I can taste test the cookie dough," Zac said.

His grandma laughed, shaking her head as they headed toward the

kitchen. They baked cookies and danced to oldies music as they waited for each batch to cook. Hearing the timer go off, they grabbed their warm cookies from the oven and headed to the table.

"Mmmmm. These are amazing! We sure are good bakers," Zac said.

"When you get your chair back, we should zoom over and deliver some to the nursing home," his grandma said.

"Why wouldn't we just take your car?" Zac asked.

4

"You know that isn't nearly as fun! I'm looking forward to my next ride on your chair. I felt like a celebrity when you drove me to dinner last week. My friends couldn't stop talking about it." Grandma laughed. "Maybe you could get a sidecar for me!" She got up and put the leftovers in the cupboard, then turned to leave.

"Bye, dearie," his grandma said, putting on her coat. "I need to run, I'm working the bingo hall tonight. I have three shifts this week."

"Bye, Grandma," Zac said as she headed to the door. "Make sure you double check the numbers B4 you call them."

His grandma giggled at the bingo joke and called over her shoulder, "Maybe I'll see you B4 my next shift."

Chapter 2

Grandma Weekend

The next morning, Zac and his mom sat glaring at each other over the kitchen table. The argument about whether he could use his Mighty Wheels at school had been raging since he got out of bed, but neither of them wanted to give in. As the time ticked by, Zac realized each second was making him later for school. He knew if he started yelling, the conversation would be over.

Taking a deep breath, he tried one final explanation.

"Mom, you *have* to let me use my Mighty Wheels for school. I can't wheel myself around all day in this old chair while carrying my books. Even before I wished in that wishing well, I had an electric wheelchair."

"You can use a backpack."

"They don't allow backpacks in classrooms."

"They will make an exception," Mom said, picking up the phone to call the school.

"But Mom, this old chair is also

7

really uncomfortable. I haven't used it in years, and I don't fit in it anymore. I can't sit in this all day. Please, I'll go straight to school and come straight home after." Zac gave his mom a sad look, hoping she would understand how he was feeling.

"Fine, but I'm driving you. You are not flying."

As his mom went to get the other chair, Zac gave a silent fist pump, grinning from ear to ear.

***

When Zac's mom pulled up in front of the school, Zac raced out of the car and into the building and saw Blake, one of his best friends, heading into science class. He caught up with him just as the bell rang.

"I like your new glasses," Blake said.

"Thanks," Zac whispered.

"Good morning," his teacher, Mrs. Kyle, said as Zac slid in behind his desk. "Before we begin, I want to hear your favorite part of the weekend."

Jasmine raised her hand. "I went to the zoo with my Nana."

Blake raised his hand next. "I played cards with my Gaga, that's what we call my grandma, and then she taught my brother and I some piano."

"I danced with my Ole'ma. She's my great-grandmother," Cynthia said.

Seeing the weekend pattern, Zac went next to talk about the cookies he baked with his grandma.

"Wow! It was quite the grandma weekend!" Mrs. Kyle exclaimed. "Even I was with my grandma Gigi this weekend! We went fishing."

Edward's shoulders slumped. "I don't have a grandma," he blurted out.

Kimi said, "I don't have a grandma either, but I went fishing with my mom."

As Mrs. Kyle and Kimi started talking about the best places to go fishing in the area, Zac noticed Edward sliding down in his chair. They weren't really friends because Edward was usually flashing around his expensive new shoes or showing off his fancy gadgets. Today was different. Zac felt a little sorry for him looking so sad and decided he would try to talk to him later.

***

"Do you smell that? Pizza day!" Zac hollered as he and Blake rushed to get in the lunch line. Zac noticed Edward on the other side of the lunchroom with his friends. *He's probably fine,* Zac thought as he grabbed some chocolate milk.

Once they got their food, Zac and Blake joined Anna, Jasmine, and Cody at their table. Jasmine was new to the school this year, but she quickly fit into the group.

"I'm grounded from flying," Zac said. "It was a challenge trying to get my mom to agree to me even using this chair for school today."

"That stinks!" Blake said. "I told Bobby you would drive him around next weekend. He loves roller

coasters, so I think he would love it." Bobby was Blake's brother, who was adopted when he was a baby. He couldn't really talk since he had an intellectual disability, but he loved playing basketball with them.

"My mom might say yes to that!"

Zac said as he bit into his pizza. "She loves Bobby!"

"Nice, using Bobby to get what *YOU* want," Anna said, rolling her eyes.

"Oh, come on. It's a win-win situation!" Cody said, giving Zac a high five.

"Do you all want to come over after school today?" Jasmine said, changing the subject. "I got a new game this weekend."

"What kind of game?" Blake asked.

"It's a virtual reality game. I got new gear for it too. You guys should come and check it out," Jasmine said.

"Are you sure you want me using that thing again?" Cody asked. "Last time I punched your TV!"

"Don't worry, this one will warn you if that's about to happen," Jasmine said. "But maybe we should put some pillows on the floor, just in case, so if you step too close to the TV, you'll know to step back."

"Ok, as long as you trust your TV's *life* around me, I'm in," Cody said with a smirk.

"My mom is picking me up, so I'll ask her if she'll drive me over," Zac said.

While he wanted to hang out with his friends, real flying was more exciting than VR. But since he wasn't able to fly right now anyway, VR would have to do.

Chapter 3

Not Rich Enough

After school, Edward dragged his feet up the stairs to his home, knowing his parents wouldn't be there to greet him. Again. When he reached the top step, he gazed out at the property. His house rose above acres of land that were cut with precision around the large garage and entry to the swimming pool. His mom had planted gardens to the left, but she never tended to them. That was the gardener's job, but she loved to show off her freshly grown tomatoes to her friends. His parents didn't seem to want to swim with him either. They were always too tired from work or too busy, even on the weekends.

If only my mom hadn't stopped talking to her mother when I was little, then maybe I would have a grandma who would garden and swim in the pool with me, Edward thought. *Maybe I could borrow someone else's grandma. Or maybe I could pay someone to be my grandma, like my nanny Mom and Dad hired when I was younger.* He had heard grandmas liked hard candy, zoos, bingo halls, baking, and fishing, but he needed to do some research.

Instead of entering the main house, Edward turned and walked to the large garage that was attached to a

guest house. As he walked through
the garage, he ran his finger along
his dad's nice cars and stopped in
front of the self-flying helicopter.
His mom's business was in self-driving
vehicles, and her company had just
developed a self-flying helicopter. Last
month, she showed him how it worked,
and they took it up for a spin. It was
really fun, but since then, she had
barely been home.

Walking out of the garage area and into the guest house, he pictured himself making cookies with his new grandma in the kitchen. It was the perfect place for a grandma to stay. She would probably like the movie theater it had also. He just had to find his new grandma. Maybe he could interview some to find the right fit.

But first, he needed a plan.

Chapter 4

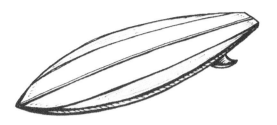

Surfboard

Zac waited outside the school until his mom pulled up. As he drove into the van, he asked, "Mom, Jasmine asked us all to come over after school. Can I go?"

"Yes, as long as you don't use your springs, fly, or use your super speed."

"So you're going to carry me up the steps like you used to do?" Zac asked with a grin. "Or can I bounce my way up?"

"Ok, ok, just don't fly," his mom said, laughing.

They drove to Jasmine's house, and

when they arrived, Zac rolled out of the van, excited to have permission to use some of his gadgets. He swung the control panel out from the side of his chair and pushed the yellow button. Springs shot out from below his chair, and he easily bounced up the steps. He had to practice that skill a lot over the summer. He would bounce up a step, and his friends would push him forward right before he fell backward. Practice makes perfect, they say.

Jasmine answered the door. "Come on in, Zac."

Cody and Blake were already there, and Blake had the VR headset on.

"I feel like I'm really flying on this skateboard!" Blake said. "Zac, I want a skateboard attached to your chair!"

"How could you attach a skateboard to my chair?" Zac asked.

"Well, it's probably impossible, but it would be really cool," Blake said.

"Nothing is impossible," Jasmine called over her shoulder as she opened the door to let Anna in.

"What's not impossible?" Anna asked when she entered the family room.

"Blake wants to attach a skateboard to my chair so he can fly with me," Zac explained.

"Well, I've flown with you before, and your robo-arm was not exactly comfortable holding me up," Blake said as he took off the VR headset.

"I agree. I felt like I was going to fall

at any moment," Cody said. "Don't get me wrong, it's so fun, but I can also see why my dad doesn't want me doing it."

"A skateboard on the side would be fun, but how would it attach to Zac's chair?" Anna asked. "The wings would be in the way."

"I've never flown with you, Zac, but what if something was attached to the back? I can ride on the back when you use superspeed and it's fine," Jasmine said.

"When he uses superspeed, the rocket boosters don't come out. When he flies, they do, so we might get burned up," Cody said.

"True," Anna said. "But if it was made of really heavy steel, couldn't it be just above the rocket boosters?"

They sat thinking for a moment, staring at Zac's chair.

"I feel like the metal could still heat up with the rocket boosters directly under it. That would make it less sturdy," Jasmine said.

"There is room in front of the wings," Cody said. "Maybe the skateboard could go there?"

"Yeah! It could be a metal piece that slides out from under Zac's chair!" Anna said, getting up to examine the chair more closely.

"How are we going to do that?" Blake asked.

"My dad has welding supplies, and I know how to weld metal together. I help him all the time," Jasmine said.

"You know how to weld? Like, how to use a blowtorch and melt the metal together?" Cody asked.

"Sure do!" Jasmine said. "Let's go in the garage and see what we can use."

23

Excited, they moved to the garage and saw a bunch of steel and aluminum against the wall, as well as steel end tables, lawn decorations, and clocks.

"Wow, this is impressive. I didn't know you and your dad did stuff like this," Cody said, admiring a flamingo lawn ornament.

"Yeah, it's fun to work with him on it," Jasmine said. "I think the stainless steel will be stronger than the aluminum, but tungsten would be even stronger. I'll ask my dad to see what he thinks. He always wants to be around when I use a blowtorch anyway."

She walked out of the garage to look for her dad while the rest of them stared at each other in awe with the new information about their friend. A minute later, her dad entered, and they got to work on Zac's chair. They developed a system where a metal board would slide in and out under his chair so his friends could stand right in front of the wing.

"My robo-arm could probably be used as a seat belt," Zac said.

"That's a good idea," Cody said. "It could loop around the rider and then latch itself to the wing."

A few hours later, it was done and ready for flight. Zac called his mom, hoping she would agree to them trying it out.

"I'll be right there," Zac's mom said.

As they waited for her to arrive,

they all went outside and took turns standing on the new invention.

"It's like a surfboard since it doesn't have wheels," Cody said. "I've always wanted to surf!"

Zac's mom arrived, quickly getting out of her car to check out the new addition.

"Let's take it up for a ride, Zac," she said. "Stay low in case it breaks."

"It's fine," Zac said. "Jasmine's dad is a professional welder."

"Great!" Zac's mom exclaimed. "That makes me feel much better."

Zac's mom stepped onto the surfboard, and Zac pulled on his glove to attach the robo-arm around her like a seat belt.

"Now you're thinking, Zac," she said. "Your extra safety feature might make me more comfortable with you

flying on your own again."

Zac smiled and hit the green button, sending them up into the air. He quickly moved the joystick to pop out the wings, staying low to the ground, and secured the robo-arm to the wing. He glanced over and saw his mom trying to hide her smile.

"Shall we go higher, Mom?" Zac asked with a smirk.

"Sure," she replied.

Zac slowly maneuvered the chair up above the trees, and his mom let out a woohoo! She always did like roller coasters. They did a spin in the air, then headed back to Jasmin's house. After everyone had a turn, including Jasmin's dad, it was decided that it was strong enough and they would be allowed to use it, as long as the seat belt was always on. They all went home energized, looking forward to their next ride on the Mighty Wheels.

Chapter 5

Ooooo, Candy!

A few days later, Edward came home from school to find his dad's big red Do Not Disturb sign on his office door again. He decided it was the perfect day to launch his plan. He went into his mom's office and grabbed the keys for the helicopter. Gathering the net and hard candies that all grandmas love, he headed out to the garage. Thankfully, the self-flying helicopter was moved from the garage, so he wouldn't have to figure out how to get it out of there. He looked down at the plan he had sketched out and decided it seemed perfect. He attached the gigantic automatic net he got from the fishing store to the bottom of the helicopter and climbed into the pilot's seat. Just three button switches later and he was up in the sky.

I'm actually doing this, Edward thought. *I can get a bunch of grandmas and find the right one to be my granny.*

He flew toward the Blinko Bingo Hall, and as he hovered above, he saw people with white hair leaving the building. *Perfect timing,* he thought. He lowered the net filled with hard candies onto the front lawn and watched with delight as the grandmas walked onto the net.

"Hey, Rosie, come here. Check out this candy. It's your favorite— caramel!" Shirley hollered over the sound of the helicopter.

As they put the candies in their mouths, the net closed around them and lifted them off the ground.

"Ooooo, a helicopter ride!" shouted Rosie as it snatched up all twenty grannies.

Edward flew back to his house and carefully lowered the grandmas so they stayed on their feet. Then he released the net and waited for them to walk out before lowering the helicopter and landing beside them.

Jumping out, he exclaimed, "Hi! Did you like the ride? Welcome to my home! You are welcome to use the garden, swimming pool, and the kitchen in the guest house, which is full of ingredients to make your favorite cookies."

"Hunky-dory!" Edna exclaimed.

"We must have won the grand prize at the Blinko Bingo Hall!" Betty yelled. There was a cheer through the crowd as they started to look around the large property.

"Who wants to make some cookies?" Edward asked. Taking a few volunteers, he skipped toward the kitchen in the guest house, ready for some granny time.

Chapter 6

No Answer

"Breaking News!" Zac heard from the TV in the family room. "Grandmas all over town are missing!"

Zac panicked and looked at his older brother Ryan. "Have you talked to Grandma today?"

"No," Ryan said, shaking his head.

Zac yelled to his mom, "Mom! Have you talked to Grandma today?"

"No, why?" she asked.

"I just heard on the news that a lot of grandmas are missing," he said as he went to get his phone from the counter.

They called his grandma—no answer. They called again—no answer.

"She's probably at the store," his mom said. "I know she worked at the bingo hall last night."

He took the cookies they made out of the cupboard and put one in his mouth. *Where could she be?* he wondered.

He picked up the phone and texted his friends. Anna, Jasmine, and Cody responded first and said their grandmas were fine. Then Blake said his grandma wasn't answering either. Since they were both worried, it was decided everyone would meet up at Zac's house.

Just then, there was a knock at the door, and Zac went to answer it. When he opened the door, Cynthia was there with her friend and

immediately started talking. Cynthia
uses a communication device, which
is a little slower than normal speech,
but Zac was used to it from being
classmates for years, so he waited
until she finished her whole sentence.

"My grandma is missing! I haven't
seen her since yesterday, and she
isn't answering the phone now. You
have to do something, Zac!"

"Did you call the police? My mom is
going to call to report my grandma
missing if we don't hear from her in a

few hours."

"Yes, we called," Cynthia said. "But I can't just sit around and wait."

Just then, Anna's mom pulled into the driveway, and Anna, Blake, and Bobby got out of the car. Cody and Jasmine raced toward them on their bikes at the same time.

Bobby walked up to Zac. "Gaga?"

"Yes, Bobby, we will try to find your Gaga," Zac said.

"Ok. Plan time," Anna said.

Zac's mom ran outside after she heard the kids arriving and sensed something was up. "What are you guys talking about out here?"

"Three of our grandmas are missing," Cynthia said. "We really need to find them."

"I'm going to drive over to my mom's house now to make sure she's not there," Zac's mom said. "Blake and Cynthia, did someone go check on yours as well?"

"Yes," Blake said. "My auntie just went over and she wasn't there."

"Mine wasn't either," Cynthia said.

"Ok. The police have been called. They will figure it out. Hold tight for now," Zac's mom said. "If we don't hear from them by tomorrow, you can discuss a plan then. I'm sure they all just went to the casino or something."

The group let out a groan as his mom headed back inside.

"Your mom is right. We shouldn't jump to conclusions," Anna said.

"But what if she's not right?" Blake asked. "Where could they be?"

Bobby grabbed Blake and pulled him toward the driveway to play basketball.

"All right, Bobby," Blake said. "I guess we can't do anything right now anyway, so we might as well play some basketball."

Chapter 7

Red Hats

Edward had fun baking cookies and watching movies with the new grandmas the night before, but he didn't think he had found his ideal granny yet. After school, he decided it was time for another trip in the helicopter.

"Grannies, I'll be back!" Edward shouted as he went outside to the helicopter.

"Did he just call us his grannies?" Beulah said, turning to Rosie. "What a silly boy."

Edward detached the net and added a huge claw the size of King Kong's hand that he'd found online. He looked at his watch. It was 4:00 p.m., so a lot of grandmas should be headed to dinner. He took off and flew the helicopter above town, looking for more grannies. Only a few miles up the road, he saw a bus with hats on the side. *Perfect,* he thought. Once when he was at the country club with his parents, a lively group of older women had walked in wearing huge hats. He'd watched them having a great time eating and laughing, and his mom had said they were part of some hat group.

Edward hovered above the bus until it stopped outside a restaurant, then he lowered the claw. "It's go time!" he yelled.

Before the bus doors could open, he pulled the bus up into the sky. It was much heavier than the bingo crowd, but he thought the helicopter could handle the short ride back to his house. He saw his swimming pool in the distance, but the helicopter began to shake, and Edward was afraid it was about to drop. He gripped the controls tightly until he reached his property, then as soon as he was in a clearing, he tried to slowly lower the bus down. It hit the ground with a thump, and the grandmas raised their hands in the air like they were on a ride! Edward landed the helicopter next to them and jumped out, thankful he made it home.

"I'm sorry about the rough ride at the end there," Edward said as

they got out of the bus. "Welcome
to my home. Come relax at the pool
or bake some lasagna with me using
tomatoes from the garden."

"That was quite a ride, sonny!"
Joyce said. She was wearing the
biggest hat Edward had ever seen.

"I think it's the most fun I've had since I was twenty!"

"Where are we?" the driver asked. She was also wearing a huge hat.

"You're on vacation!" Edward said. "Just call me grandson and enjoy yourself."

Slightly confused, the grandmas looked at each other, but then Joyce laughed and hollered, "Well then, just call me Meema!"

They all laughed, and Edward started showing them around, introducing them to the bingo grandmas. With this many grandmas at his house, he figured it was time to let the town know they were safe and he was just doing some interviews.

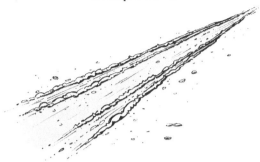

Chapter 8

Helicopter Skids

Zac got home from school and immediately turned on the TV.

"Breaking News!" the news reporter said. "More grandmas are missing."

"Mom! Come quick!" Zac yelled as he moved closer to the TV.

His mom ran into the room and stared at the screen. "This time, we believe a bus of older women wearing hats was taken."

"I'm worried, Mom," Zac said.

"Me too," she admitted.

"We received this video just moments ago," the reporter continued as a video of a masked person came on the screen.

Zac hit the record button on the remote in case there were any clues. The TV would be much easier to see than looking on his small phone.

"Your grandmothers are fine and in good hands. They are having more fun than they have ever had with their own grandchildren." The video ended.

"That is the only information we have at this time. The police are investigating," the reporter explained. "We will keep you up to date on the findings."

Zac texted his friends to get to his house right away. Within minutes, they were sitting around his living room watching the recording.

"Did you see what was in the background of the video? It's the water tower. That's not far from here," Zac said.

Looking at Zac's mom, Blake begged, "Can Zac please fly his Mighty Wheels to help find our grandmas?"

"You know what happened last time you flew, Zac," his mom said, looking him in the eyes. "You weren't paying attention and almost flew into a telephone wire. Those birds that flew at you may have actually saved your life."

"You're right, Mom," Zac said.

"Can you promise me you will be more careful and watch where you are going at all times?"

"Yes, I promise," Zac replied.

"Ok, you can go. I will drive Anna, Jasmine, and Cody and meet you there. But you know the rules. You cannot be alone, and you must have your friends with you," his mom said. "And call the police if you see anything before we get there."

"Thanks, Mom," Zac said, relieved. "First stop is the water tower."

Blake and Zac went outside while his mom looked for her car keys. Blake extended the surfboard from under Zac's chair and climbed on. Pulling on the glove, Zac extended the robo-arm around him.

"You good?" Zac asked. "Does it feel tight enough?"

"Yes, but after you take off, let's see if it will stay in place if you take the glove off without retracting the arm back in," Blake said. "You may need both hands soon."

Zac pressed the green button, shooting the rocket boosters out, and launched them into the air. Zac attached the robo-arm to the wing, then slowly took off the glove and put it back in its holder. He was surprised when the arm stayed in place. "Great idea! I didn't know it could do that!"

Blake was happy to have the seat belt as Zac shot up into the sky.

The police were leaving just as Zac and Blake landed near the water tower.

Zac retracted the robo-arm, and Blake quickly stepped off the board and pushed it under the chair. "Wow, we built that really well."

"Next, you guys will probably want a sidecar on the other side like my grandma does," Zac said with a smirk.

"That's a great idea!" Blake said. "With heat and air conditioning. Now you're talking comfort!"

They laughed as they looked around at their surroundings.

"I guess the police saw the same thing we did," Zac said, watching their cars head back down the road. "Let's look around and see if we can find any clues."

They had just started exploring when Zac's friends and mom arrived.

"Did you guys find anything?" Jasmine asked as she got out of the car.

"No, not yet," Zac said.

"Maybe we should look where the police haven't," Anna said. "I noticed a clearing when we pulled up. Follow me."

Zac's mom stayed to look at the area where the video was taken, and the friends followed Anna, who led them into the woods. They walked for about five minutes until Anna pointed to the clearing up ahead.

"Look at this," Blake said when they arrived. He was pointing down at two long lines in the dirt.

"It looks like landing skids on a

helicopter," Cody said. They all turned to him with confused looks on their faces.

"I like airplanes and stuff," Cody said. "You guys know that. What's the big deal?"

"We've just never heard of landing skids before," Blake said. "But yeah, that would make sense."

"Why would a helicopter land around here?" Cody continued. "The airport is miles away."

"Yeah, I wonder if that's a clue,"

Anna said.

"Oh, it's a clue," Cody said. "This has to be our guy."

"Why do you think it's a guy? The masked person didn't show their face or much of their body," Anna said.

"True," Jasmine said. "And it sounded like one of those voice changer things were used."

"Fine, this has got to be our *person*," Cody said. "It just doesn't sound like a villain then."

"Maybe we can look up who has helicopters in the area. They have to be registered, right?" Blake asked, turning the talk back to the case of the missing grannies.

"Good idea. Let's do a final sweep to make sure there aren't any more clues before we leave," Zac said as he slowly drove around the area.

After looking around and coming up empty-handed, they headed back to the water tower.

"Did you find anything?" Anna asked Zac's mom.

"No. You?" she answered.

"We think the person who created the video came over here in a helicopter," Anna said.

"Interesting," Zac's mom said. "Let's go and see the latest news reports and see if anything new has been discovered. We may need to call the police with this information."

Chapter 9

A Closer Look

The next day, Zac stayed home from school with his brother Ryan. He was too worried about his grandma to think about school. His friends had found all the people who had registered helicopters, including some local companies. The only one he recognized was Edward's mom's company. He had heard him talking about cars before, but not helicopters. Zac decided he would fly past them all and see if anything looked suspicious, but he had to wait for his friends to get out of school. In the meantime, he mapped out the route. He left the news on just in case anything came up about the missing grandmas. His mom had to go to work, and she'd made him promise he would call the police if he saw anything suspicious.

In the background, he heard it again. "Breaking News!"

"Ryan, it's on the news! Come here!" Zac yelled, rushing to the TV to hit record on the remote so he could show his friends whatever was about to happen. Ryan ran into the room, throwing himself on the couch.

"We have received a new video of the person who claims to have the missing grandmothers," the news reporter said. "We have been unable

to track the message that was
sent, but the police are examining
it and are confident they will find
the grandmas soon. Here is the new
video."

"I've seen the news," the masked
person said, "and I know people are
worried about their grandmas. There
is nothing to worry about, as I stated
before. They are safe and having
fun. The interview process will be
over soon, and the grannies will be

returned." The video ended, and the reporter returned to the screen.

"Interview process?" Zac said. "What does that mean?"

"I don't know. It really doesn't make sense," Ryan said.

"I think we should go look for this person now. Will you go with me?" Zac asked.

"I can't. I have soccer practice soon," he said. "Besides, the police are handling it."

Knowing soccer was a new sport for his brother, and he had been nervous about it, Zac didn't bug him any further. He waited impatiently until his friends knocked on the door after school.

"You have to see this!" Zac said as Blake, Anna, Jasmine, and Cody sat down to watch the TV. Zac played the recording of the masked person.

"Play it again!" Cody said when the recording ended.

They played it over and over, looking for clues. This time, the video seemed to be taken from inside a room of a house.

Suddenly, Blake jumped up out of his seat. "Wait! Pause it!" he yelled as he ran up to the TV. He pointed at the screen and said, "What is THAT?!"

"Is it an envelope attached to the fridge?" Cody asked.

"It might be! Let me see if I can find this video on my phone," Anna said and quickly searched for the Local 4 News video. "I've found it! I'll screenshot it so I can zoom in."

As Anna zoomed in, her friends

squeezed in beside her to try to see.

"Is that an address?" Cody asked. "Didn't this person's parents teach them anything about internet safety?"

"It's really hard to see, but it definitely says Lake Lawson," Jasmine said.

"I have one of those magnifier apps. Let me try it," Cody said and pulled out his phone to hold it next to Anna's. "I think it says Goodale. That's further out of town, where all the expensive houses are."

"Ok, let's go!" Zac said as he sped toward the door.

"Wait! We need a plan, and we can't all fit on your wheelchair!" Anna shouted.

"We do need a sidecar!" Blake said. "Anna, can

you call your dad or mom and ask them to drive you guys out there? Zac and I can fly around and will text you when we find the house."

"Sounds like a plan. And you need to call the police when you find the house," Anna said.

"Of course," Zac said. "I'm not crazy. We don't know who we are dealing with."

"What about me?!" Cody whined. "Blake got to go with you last time, Zac!"

"My grandma is MISSING, Cody!" Blake yelled.

Cody calmed down, realizing how worried Blake was. "Ok, ok. We will meet you there."

Zac and Blake headed to the door while Anna picked up her phone to call her parents.

Chapter 10

Behind the Mask

Zac and Blake headed north toward
Goodale Street. Zac was starting to
worry, wondering what he might find.
Was his grandma really ok, and was
this person really just interviewing
her? What did that even mean? Why
would anyone interview a grandma?
Zac soon found Goodale, though,
and his thoughts turned to looking
at each house carefully, slowly flying
over each one and searching for any

sign of the missing grannies.

"What are we looking for?" Blake yelled to Zac over the wind.

"I don't know, but with over fifty missing grandmas, we should see some, don't you think?" Zac hollered back.

He was nearing the end of the street when he flew over a huge property. Instantly, he spotted a swimming pool with a bunch of older women in hats sitting around it. Zac hovered above the trees so they could study the people more closely. They were definitely grannies! They continued to scan the property and saw a bus parked in the back.

"This has got to be it!" Zac said. "I'll try to find a place to land where they can't see us."

Zac went further into the woods and lowered them down as softly as he could.

"You're not going to believe this, but I've been here before," Blake whispered, getting off the board. "I came to a birthday party here when I was seven. It's Edward's house."

"Really?! That's crazy! Do you remember that day in class when everyone was talking about their grandmas?" Zac asked.

"Yeah," Blake replied, looking confused.

"Edward said he didn't have one. It was the first time I ever saw him look sad," Zac said, realizing he should have talked to Edward that day.

"So he thought stealing grandmas was the way to get what he wanted?" Blake said, shaking his head. "Oh, and the helicopter skids! You told me that Edward's mom had a registered helicopter. It all makes sense now!"

Zac grabbed his phone out of his jacket pocket and called the police, giving them the location. Then he called Anna and told her the news.

"There is a big fire on the other side of town. It's just in a field, but it may take a while for the police to get

over there. Be careful," Anna said.

Feeling relieved that it was probably just Edward, Zac and Blake decided to investigate. They walked up to the pool and scanned the faces of the ladies who were sitting around chatting. Their grandmas were nowhere to be seen. But Edward was there. He was in the pool playing catch with one woman and looking happier than Zac had ever seen him. Until he saw Zac.

Edward stopped smiling and got out of the pool. He grabbed his towel and shirt, opened the gate, and walked over to them.

"What are YOU doing here?" Edward snarled.

"Looking for our grandmas," Zac said. "Where are they? We know they are here somewhere."

"I don't know what you are talking about," Edward said.

"Then you won't mind me looking around," Blake said and headed off to the house.

"You go that way, Blake, and I'll head to the garage," Zac said.

But before Zac could move an inch, Edward jumped in front of him.

"You're welcome to check out the house, but my dad has all his nice cars in the garage and won't let anyone near them," Edward said.

Blake turned around and got on the

back of Zac's wheelchair and said,
"Thanks for the hint, Edward. Zac,
shall we?"

Without another word, Zac shot up
in the air, bouncing over Edward to

the door of the garage. Edward took off running behind them. As soon as they reached the door, Zac grabbed the handle, but it was locked.

"Release the grandmas!" Zac shouted.

"No way!" Edward reached into a pocket on his shirt, pulled out a stack of one-hundred-dollar bills, and began waving it toward Zac. "Leave now and all this is yours."

"No amount of money could bribe me into leaving my grandma in your hands," Zac said. "Where is she?"

Edward started folding one of the one-hundred-dollar bills into a star at lightning speed. "They are safe and happy with me."

"Do you really think they are happy being locked up without their grandchildren?" Blake asked.

"I'm their grandchild now," Edward said, continuing to fold up the money into stars.

"It doesn't seem like the time to be making origami, but it is impressive. How did you learn that?" Zac asked.

"Expensive paper throwing lessons," Edward said with an evil grin as he took a step forward and threw the first star at Zac.

"Ow!" Zac cried as the money star sliced into his arm.

"Run!" Zac yelled to Blake as stars shot toward them.

Just then, Anna's mom's truck pulled into the driveway. Edward saw his opportunity, unlocked the door to the garage, and hurried inside.

Anna's mom, Anna, Cody, and Jasmine climbed out of the truck, and Zac quickly filled them in on what had happened so far.

"This is ridiculous. Isn't there an adult in this house? Where are his parents? Or a butler or someone? I'm going to the main house. There has to be an adult here." She took off in the direction of the main house.

"How do we get in?" Cody asked.

"The door seems to be made of metal, so it would hurt pretty bad to ram into it at super speed. But there is an opening at the top. Maybe my robo-arm could go through there and then go down to reach the door handle on the other side." Zac put on his glove and extended the arm, easily reaching through the gap at the top, but the tough part would be guiding his arm into place without seeing the other side of the door. Bending his real arm down so the

robo-arm would copy, he moved his arm lower so it was directly above where he thought the handle would be. He moved his fingers around, trying to feel something. The doorknob was there. Searching around it, he felt a bump and moved it to the right, hoping it was the lock. Click.

"Yes! That's it!" Cody whispered.

"Let's go save some grannies!"

They slowly walked into the garage, and immediately paper stars started flying at them.

Blake, Anna, and Jasmine slid under a table as Cody grabbed the nearest garbage can lid to protect his face.

Zac quickly pushed the yellow button on his Mighty Wheels and bounced out of the way. As he bounced up, he noticed security cameras behind Edward and saw his grandma in what looked like a kitchen. Determined to save his grandma, he bounced back toward Blake and Anna.

"The grandmas are on the other side of the garage in the guest house. You need to get to them," Zac whispered to Blake and Anna as he bounced down.

"But how? We need a distraction," Blake said.

"I'll take care of that," Zac said.

He pushed the red stop button on his panel and landed back on the ground, then he quickly extended his robo-arm toward Edward across the room.

"You should have taken the money," Edward said. He ran to a wall full of buttons, hit a few of them, then ran toward the door at the opposite end of the garage.

Lights flashed! Hearing a creaking noise above, Zac looked up. A red car was shaking directly above him. Before he had time to move out of the way, it dropped. Zac thought fast and extended his powerful robo-arm up, catching the car just in time. The robo-hand shook as it took on the weight, so Zac threw it into the side of the building, creating a huge hole.

"Now!" Zac yelled to his friends.

"But what about Edward? He's escaping!" Anna said.

"We will get him. Go save the grandmas!" Zac yelled.

Chapter 11

Grandma's Little Eddie

Edward sprinted out of the garage, but Zac was faster. Using his robo-arm, he grabbed Edward just as he was about to get into the helicopter.

"It's over, Edward," Zac said.

"That's pretty obvious, isn't it?" Edward said with a bored look on his face.

"I can't believe you did this. Didn't you think we would be worried about our grandmas?" Blake asked.

"Worried? Why would anyone need

to worry? Do you see any grandmas screaming? They were having a great time. They think they won a vacation," Edward said. "Besides, who wouldn't want to live here?"

Zac looked at Cody and said, "He honestly doesn't think he did anything wrong."

"Do you know how scared you have made this whole town? Do you know how scared Blake, Cynthia, and Zac were, thinking their grandmas got kidnapped?" Cody yelled.

"You thought they were kidnapped?" Edward asked, looking concerned for the first time. "I didn't realize that. I borrowed them so I could find my ideal grandma. You know, interview them all until I found my match."

"Edward! What have you done?!" Edward's dad came running out of the house screaming. As he ran down the long driveway toward the garage, police cars suddenly pulled in. "I thought you were just playing with your friends out here the last few days, but I've just been told you have kidnapped GRANDMOTHERS?!"

Just then, a police officer came up to them, and Zac handed Edward over to him.

"This is who took all the grandmas, officer," Zac said. "There are more grannies by the pool and in the guest house."

"Thank you for your help," the police officer said as he took hold of Edward and led him toward the police car. Edward's dad followed close behind, trying to tell the officer it was all a misunderstanding.

"Grandma!" Zac yelled as the grandmas started coming out of the

guest house. He zoomed over to her and gave her the hardest hug she'd ever felt.

"What are you doing here, Zac?" his grandma asked. "Are you friends with little Eddie?"

"No, and if I was, I wouldn't be anymore," Zac said. "Did you not realize we have been looking for you for two days?"

"Oh my!" his grandma said, surprised. "I don't take my phone to the bingo hall, and that's where my vacation began, so I didn't know you were calling."

Zac told his grandma and all the grannies listening exactly what went on the last few days. They were all worried for "little Eddie" and concerned about what would happen to him.

Chapter 12

Giants or Gorillas

Zac, his mom, and his brother Ryan sat down for dinner after a long day in court. The grandmas didn't want to press charges because they had a good time and thought it was a big misunderstanding.

"Can you believe Edward just has to do community service?" Zac asked.

"Well, it is every week for the next three years, so they are taking it seriously," his mom said.

"It's crazy, actually! He has to volunteer at the old folk's home!" Ryan said, laughing.

"It's called an assisted living facility," Zac's mom said with a stern look.

"Ok, but it's still funny he has to volunteer at the assisted living facility," Ryan said. "He will probably love it."

"He did give quite a speech today about how sorry he was for taking the grandmas. And that part about how he didn't understand before that bragging about his expensive gadgets could make other people feel bad," Zac said. "He understood being jealous for the first time. But I'm still very mad at him."

"It's ok to be mad at the situation, but you should still forgive him. It only hurts you more when you don't, and you don't want that in your heart," his mom said. "He also has to go to counseling with his whole family, which I think will help. I do feel a bit bad for him that his parents are never around and he doesn't see his grandparents."

"Yeah, that is true. He was always bragging, so I never realized he cared about anything other than money," Zac said thoughtfully.

"This has been a crazy couple of months!" Ryan said, "First the Wishing Well, then the Giant, then the Missing Grannies. What will be next?!"

"Maybe it will be aliens like you said last time!" Zac's mom said.

"Or maybe a giant gorilla will escape from the zoo. Or maybe someone else gets superpowers!" Zac said.

"I do like gorillas, but can we make it chimpanzees? They seem more fun," his mom said, laughing.

"I guess someone else with superpowers isn't realistic. Last month, we went back to the well and it had disappeared," Zac said sadly.

"Oh, like aliens are realistic?!" Ryan said. "Of course, who would have thought we would have had a case of the missing grannies in our small town either."

They laughed as they gobbled up their food, each wondering what the next adventure could be.

About the Authors

Andrea Kurth is a special education teacher from Michigan who realized her students weren't often represented in books and wanted to change that. Inspired by her students, she set out to create a fun series where the story is the focus, not the disability, and is filled with adventure for younger children but exciting enough for the older struggling reader. Everyone should be represented in books. When Andrea isn't teaching or writing, she enjoys traveling with her wonderful husband and sons. Visit her at www.kurthbooks.com to connect and for free lesson plans.

Braden Kurth is a high school student who enjoys hanging out with friends and family, playing video games, and many other things. He aspires to be an entrepreneur.

About the Illustrator

Justin Rose is an illustrator and graphic designer from Michigan. His work includes children's books, editorial illustration, caricatures, paintings and graphic design. His goal is to use his talent for the good of the community, and to put as many smiles on as many faces as possible. See more of his work at www.justinrose.net.

Made in United States
North Haven, CT
22 January 2023

31451639R00061